Hairs · Pelitos

by Sandra Cisneros · illustrated by Terry Ybáñez

TRES FLORES

three flowers
BRILLIANTINE
CONTAINS:
PETROLATUM,
FRAGRANCE
3¼ OZ. NET WT.

DRAGONFLY BOOKS ⤙⟶⟵ NEW YORK

Para los kids,

Aleksandra,
Alfredito,
Alain,
Alonso,
Paolo,
Alexandro,
y Arturito

—S. C.

Para mis estudiantes de Travis
Elementary en San Antonio, Tejas

—T. Y.

Translated from the English by Liliana Valenzuela

Traducción al español por Liliana Valenzuela

Everybody in our family has different hair.

Todos en nuestra familia tenemos pelo diferente.

My papa's hair is like a broom,

El pelo de mi papá es como una escoba,

all up in the air.

todo parado de punta.

And me, my hair is lazy.

Y yo, mi pelo es flojo.

It never obeys barrettes or bands.

Nunca obedece a broches o diademas.

Carlos's hair is thick and straight.

El pelo de Carlos es grueso y lacio.

He doesn't need to comb it.

No necesita peinárselo.

Nenny's hair is slippery—

El pelo de Nenny es resbaloso—

slides out of your hand.

se escurre de tu mano.

And Kiki, who is youngest,

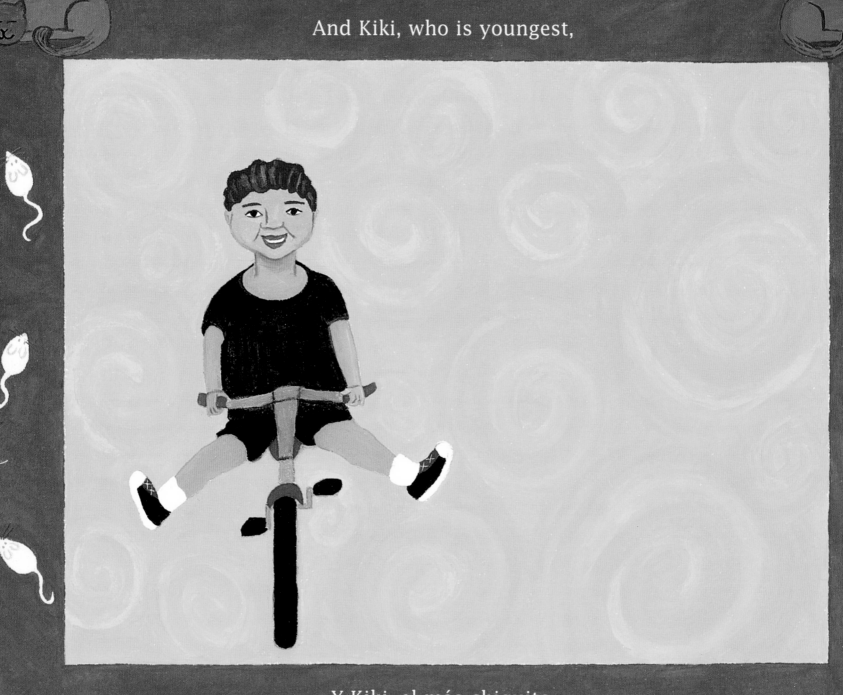

Y Kiki, el más chiquito,

has hair like fur.

tiene pelo como peluche.

But my mother's hair, my mother's hair, like little rosettes,

Pero el pelo de mi mamá, el pelo de mi mamá, como rositas,

like little candy circles, all curly and pretty because

como rueditas de dulce, todas chinitas y lindas porque

she pinned it in pin curls all day,

se hizo anchoas con pasadores todo el día,

sweet to put your nose into when she is holding you,

dulce cuando pones tu nariz en él cuando ella te abraza,

holding you and you feel safe,

cuando te abraza y te sientes segura,

is the warm smell of bread before you bake it,

es el olor tibio a pan antes de hornearlo,

is the smell when she makes room for you

es el olor cuando te hace un campito

on her side of the bed still warm with her skin,

en su lado de la cama todavía calientito de su piel,

and you sleep near her,

y te duermes cerca de ella,

the rain outside falling and Papa snoring.

la lluvia cayendo afuera y Papá roncando.

The snoring, the rain, and Mama's hair that smells like bread.

Los ronquidos, la lluvia, y el pelo de Mamá que huele a pan.

All rights reserved. Published in the United States by Dragonfly Books, an imprint of
Random House Children's Books, a division of Random House, Inc., New York. The text of this work
was originally published as part of the collection *The House on Mango Street*, by Arte Publico Press, Houston, in 1984.
Published in hardcover in the United States by Alfred A. Knopf, an imprint of Random House Children's Books,
a division of Random House, Inc., New York, in 1994.

Dragonfly Books with the colophon is a registered trademark of Random House, Inc.

Visit us on the Web! www.randomhouse.com/kids

Educators and librarians, for a variety of teaching tools, visit us at
www.randomhouse.com/teachers

The Library of Congress has cataloged the hardcover edition of this work as follows:

Cisneros, Sandra.
Hairs = Pelitos / by Sandra Cisneros ; illustrated by Terry Ybáñez.
p. cm.
Summary: A child describes how each person in the family has hair that looks and
acts different, Papa's like a broom, Kiki's like fur, and Mama's with the smell of warm bread.
ISBN 978-0-679-86171-3 (trade) — ISBN 978-0-679-96171-0 (lib. bdg.)
[1. Hair—Fiction. 2. Hispanic Americans—Fiction. 3. Spanish language materials—Bilingual.]
I. Ybáñez, Terry, ill. II. Title. III. Title: Pelitos.
PZ73.C53   1994   93032775

ISBN 978-0-679-89007-2 (pbk.)

MANUFACTURED IN CHINA
29 28 27 26 25 24 23 22 21

Random House Children's Books supports the First Amendment and celebrates the right to read.